CHILDREN'S CLASSICS

Peter Pan

By
James Matthew Barrie

Adapted by
Mary Kerr

Edited by
Sophie Evans

Published by BK Books Ltd
First published in 2007
Copyright © BK Books Ltd

ISBN: 978-1-906068-45-5
Printed in China

Contents

Contents

Chapter 1

The Family

Mrs. Darling had three children Wendy, John and Michael. She was a most kind and loving mother. The children had one of the prettiest nurseries in the world. They loved their mother so much that they didn't go to sleep till they had heard a lovely song from her.

The Darlings were poor. Mrs. Darling was content with things as they were in her household, but Mr. Darling had a habit of

being exactly like his neighbors. Therefore, in spite of limited resources, they had appointed a nurse for the children.

Their nurse, however, was quite different from the other nurses. Her name was Nana. You see, what distinguished her from the other nurses, was the fact that Nana was a dog, a prim Newfoundland dog. Nana was quite a treasure as a nurse. She was up at even the slightest cry of the children. She escorted the children to school, walking quietly by their side, but if they strayed from the line it was her job to put them back.

In a sentence, it can be said that the children loved Nana and Nana loved the children. Mr. Darling believed that no nursery could be so well conducted as theirs. And it was all because of Nana. Yet, there was one thing that troubled him and it was that Nana *didn't like him*. Mrs. Darling tried to assure him, by saying, "I know she admires you tremendously, George". The children would try to cheer up their father by dancing around him. I can't think of a happier family than that of the Darlings.

It's rightly said that the age of happiness is short; all things changed with the arrival of Peter Pan.

That night happened to be Nana's evening off. After putting the children to sleep, Mrs. Darling sat down by the fire to sew. But soon she drifted off to sleep in the chair beside the fireplace.

Suddenly, the window of the nursery blew open and a boy dropped on the floor. Mrs. Darling was awakened by this sudden "thump" on the floor and was surprised to see a little boy. He was a lovely boy, dressed in a suit of green leaves and a light followed him wherever he moved.

But the most captivating thing about him was that he had all his first teeth. This boy was Peter Pan, the boy who did not want to grow up. When Peter saw that Mrs. Darling was a grown-up, he gnashed his little pearls at her. Mrs. Darling screamed in fright.

Chapter 2

Peter Arrives

Hearing Mrs. Darling's scream, Nana entered the room. She growled and sprang at the boy, who immediately leapt out of the window. Mrs. Darling let out a cry again, this time in distress for the boy, as she thought he was killed. She ran down the street to look for his little body but was unable to find it.

When Mrs. Darling returned to the nursery, she saw Nana clutching something in her mouth. It came out be Peter Pan's shadow. When Peter Pan had leapt at the window, Nana had run towards it and quickly closed it. Though Peter managed to escape, his shadow had got trapped. 'Slam!' went the window, and snapped Peter's shadow off.

Mrs. Darling examined the shadow carefully, but she found nothing extraordinary about it. Nana knew very well what to do with it. She was sure the boy would be back for his shadow, so she hung it out of the window. She put the shadow where he could get it easily without disturbing the children. Mrs. Darling didn't want the shadow to hang out of the window. She thought it looked like clothes hung out for drying, and most importantly, it spoils the look of the house. Therefore, Mrs. Darling thought to keep it in the drawer, until she found the right opportunity to tell her husband.

She found the opportunity a week later on

that 'never-to-be-forgotten Friday.' "I ought to have been especially careful on a Friday," Mrs. Darling used to say afterwards to her husband. "No, no," Mr. Darling always said, "I am responsible for it. I, George Darling, did it." Thus, they sat and recalled the incidents of that dreadful Friday, till every detail of it was embossed on their brains. "If only I had not gone to dine at no 27," said Mrs. Darling.

"If only I had not made the mistake of pouring medicine in Nana's bowl," said Mr. Darling. "If only I had pretended to like the medicine," was what Nana's wet eyes expressed. "My liking for parties, George," Mrs. Darling would cry.

"My fatal gift of humor, dearest," Mr. Darling would lament. Nana would lament sometimes too, thinking, "It's true, a dog nurse can't be efficient, they should have kept a proper nurse."

Many a time Mr. Darling would sit with Nana in the empty nursery recalling every single detail of that dreadful evening.

It seemed to be a usual Friday evening, which had begun with Nana carrying Michael on her back for the bath.

"I won't go to bed so early!" little Michael had shouted, like the person who believes that his word is final on the subject.

"I won't! I won't! Nana, it isn't six o'clock yet. I tell you I won't be bathed, I won't, I won't!" continued Michael.

At that moment, Mrs. Darling had entered the room, wearing her white evening gown which Wendy loved. She was happy to see the children playing with Nana.

Mr. Darling went on with the recollections of the evening.

"It was then when I had rushed like a cyclone in to the room, wasn't it?" Mr. Darling would thus scorn himself.

He was not wrong in comparing himself to a cyclone. He had to go to the party that evening. All was well with him till he came to his tie. Though Mr. Darling knew everything about stocks and shares, he was unable to learn the art of tying the tie.

He came rushing into the nursery with the little tie in his hand.

"What's the matter dear?" Mrs. Darling inquired.

"Matter!" he yelled, "This tie, it will not tie." Mrs. Darling was busy with the children, so she didn't pay attention to Mr. Darling's trifling about his tie. When Mr. Darling saw that his wife was not paying heed to his words, he went on sternly, "I am telling you Mrs. Darling, that unless this tie is round my neck, we are not going out for dinner. And if I don't go out to dinner tonight, I will never go to the office again. My not going to the office will bring us on the street.

Mrs. Darling remained calm. "Let me try, dear," she said.

This was what Mr. Darling really wanted. With her nice cool hands, she tied the tie for him, while the children stood around to see their fate decided. As soon as the tie was round his neck, Mr. Darling's anger evaporated. The next moment, he was dancing round the room with the little ones.

The evening witnessed another argument but this time it was over the medicine. Mr. Darling was brave, but as far as the medicine was concerned, he behaved rather oddly. If in some moment he felt weak, he consoled himself by saying, 'How can I be weak, when I can have even the bitter medicine.' So, when Michael refused to take the medicine and dodged the spoon in Nana's mouth, he said reprovingly, "Be a man, Michael." "I will not have that medicine, no, no." Michael cried naughtily. "That medicine you sometimes take, father, is much nastier, isn't it?" Wendy said to encourage Michael. "It's really bad, much nastier than Michael's," Mr. Darling said bravely. To settle the argument, Wendy

suggested, "Why don't both of you take it at the same time?" "Definitely!" said Mr. Darling. "So, are you ready, Michael?" "One, two, three," Wendy counted and Michael took the medicine. But Mr. Darling hid his medicine behind his back. Michael was disappointed with this action of his father. "O father!" exclaimed Wendy. "What do you mean by 'O father'?" Mr. Darling demanded. "Stop that, Michael, I meant to drink it, but I ... I missed it." It was dreadful the way all the three children were looking at Mr. Darling. Their glance made him shameful of what he had done.

"Look kids, I have thought of a splendid joke. I shall pour the medicine into Nana's bowl; she will drink it, thinking it as milk," Mr. Darling said.

The children were not impressed by this idea; none the less, they looked at him reproachfully as Mr. Darling poured the medicine into Nana's bowl.

When Nana came in, Mr. Darling said, "Nana I have poured some milk into your bowl."

Nana loved milk; she ran to the bowl and started lapping up its contents. Then she gave Mr. Darling such a look which, surely, was not an angry look. There were tears shining in her eyes. Without saying anything she crept into her kennel.

The children felt sorry to see their nurse so depressed. Then Wendy ran and hugged Nana. At this, Mr. Darling grew angry. He shouted, "That's right, pamper her, love her, no one loves me! Oh dear no! I am the sole breadwinner, then also why should I be loved – why, why, why!" "George," Mrs. Darling pleaded, "Don't shout! The neighbors will hear you." "Let them hear!" he answered recklessly. "Let the whole world hear. But I will no longer allow a dog to rule my nursery."

Mr. Darling was firm in his decision; crying children didn't melt his heart. He dragged Nana from the nursery and tied her up in the back-yard. But, after that, he was so ashamed that he went and sat in the passage, weeping.

Meanwhile, Mrs. Darling put the children to bed. That night, sleep didn't want to touch the children's eyes; they heard Nana barking. John whispered,

"It is because father has chained her up in the yard." But Wendy was clever. "Nana is not barking because she is sad, that is her bark when she smells danger," she said.

Mrs. Darling trembled with fear; she checked whether the windows were safely bolted or not. Everything was fine but then also her heart was in the grip of an unknown fear. "Oh, how I wish that I wasn't going to a party tonight!"

Before leaving, Mrs. Darling kissed the little foreheads. Little Michael threw his arms around her and said; "Mother, I love you." These were the last words that Mrs. Darling heard from her children.

Mr. and Mrs. Darling left for the party at number 27, which was not far away from the house. They walked down the road which was covered with snow. They were the only people in the street, and all the stars were watching them.

Stars are beautiful, but they were not friendly to Peter, who had a mischievous way of hiding behind them and troubling them. They were fun-loving; therefore tonight, they were on the side of Peter. So, as soon as the door of no. 27 closed on Mr. and Mrs. Darling, there was a tumult in the sky, and even the smallest star in the sky screamed out, "Now, Peter!"

Chapter 3

Away! Away!

All was right while Mr. and Mrs Darling were in the house. But as soon as they left, things started acting unusually. The three night-lights by the beds of the three children were burning clearly. Suddenly, Wendy's light blinked and gave a tremendous yawn. The other two followed, and before they could close their mouths, all three went off.

But the room didn't sink in the darkness; there was a new light in the room, which was one thousand times brighter than the night lights burning in the room. It moved from one corner to the other corner. If you would have looked at it carefully, you could have seen a figure, no bigger than your hand.

It was Tinker Bell, the fairy, dressed in a gown of leaves. She was searching all the drawers in the nursery and rummaging in the wardrobe, for Peter's shadow.

A moment later, the window blew open and Peter Pan dropped in.

"Tinker Bell," he called softly, "did you find my shadow?"

Tinker, in her fairy language, told Peter that his shadow was in the chest of drawers. Peter jumped at the drawer. After scattering its contents on the floor, he recovered his shadow. Peter was so delighted to have found it that he forgot that he had shut Tinker Bell up in the drawer.

Peter believed that if a man's shadow is brought near him, it at once joins the

person. But when this didn't happen, he was shocked. Then he tried to stick his shadow on with soap from the bathroom; but this too failed. A shudder passed through him, he sat on the floor and started crying. Wendy was woken up by his sobs. She sat up, and instead of being alarmed, she was pleasantly interested in him and his grief.

"Boy," she said politely, "why are you crying?" Peter could be polite, when he wanted to. Peter could also be exceedingly polite; he had learned his manners from the fairies. He rose and bowed to Wendy beautifully. Wendy was much pleased, and returned the bow.

"What's your name?" he asked. "My name is Wendy Moira Angela Darling," she replied. "What is your name?" "I am Peter Pan." "Is that all?" said Wendy. "Yes," he said rather sharply. It was the first time Peter had felt that his name was quite short.

"I'm sorry if I hurt you," said Wendy. "It doesn't matter," Peter gulped. "Where do you stay, Peter Pan?" "Second to the right," said Peter, "and then straight on till morning." "What a funny address it is!" "No, it isn't," Peter replied angrily. "What I mean," Wendy said nicely, "is, what address do people put on the letters?" If only Wendy had not mentioned letters to Peter.

"No one writes letters to me," he said contemptuously. "But your mother must be getting letters?" "I don't have a mother," he said. Wendy felt that she was standing in the middle of a tragedy.

"O Peter, that must be the reason for your crying", she said, getting out of the bed and running to him. "I wasn't crying for my mother," he said rather indignantly. "I was crying because I can't get my shadow to stick on. Besides, I wasn't crying!" "Has it come off?" "Yes." Wendy noticed the shadow lying on the floor.

"It is awful!" she exclaimed. But she could not help smiling when she saw that he had been trying to stick it on with soap. How exactly like a boy! Wendy was a clever girl; she knew exactly what to do.

"I shall sew it on for you," she said. Then, she bought the sewing bag and started sewing the shadow on Peter's foot.

"I daresay it will hurt a little," she warned him. "Oh, I will not cry," said Peter, clenching his teeth. "It would have been better if I had ironed it," Wendy said, when she had finished sewing. But Peter, like all boys, was indifferent to the appearances. He was now jumping about in the wildest glee. He had forgotten that without Wendy's help, he couldn't have got his shadow back. He thought that he had attached the shadow himself. "How clever I am!" he cried happily.

Wendy was shocked. "If I have been of no use, it's better to leave," she exclaimed, and went back to her bed and covered her face with the blanket.

Peter was bewildered. "Wendy!" he cried, "Do not be upset. I can't help boasting, when I am happy. I know that one girl is better than twenty boys." Peter was very clever in saying this. With these words, Wendy's anger evaporated, and she peeped out of the bed-clothes. "Do you really mean it, Peter?" "Yes, I do." "It's really sweet of you to think so", she said. She also said that she would give him a kiss if he liked, but Peter didn't know the meaning of a kiss. So, he held out his hand expectantly. "Do you know what a kiss is?" she asked. "I shall know when you give it to me," he replied stiffly. Wendy did not want to hurt his feelings, so she gave him a thimble. "Now, it's my turn. Shall I give you a kiss?" he said. "If you please," she replied. Peter gave her an acorn button, which she promised to put around her neck. It was lucky that she did put it on with the chain, for it afterwards saved her life. Peter and Wendy then resumed their conversation.

"I don't know," he replied uneasily, "but I think I am quite young. I started running the day I was born." Wendy was quite surprised and asked, "But, why did you run?" "Because I heard my father and mother," continued Peter, "talking about

what I was to be when I became a man." Peter looked agitated now. "I don't ever want to be a man," he said. "I want to remain a little boy, so I ran away to Kensington Gardens and have lived for a long time with the fairies." Wendy was impressed to hear that Peter knew fairies. She shot various questions about them at Peter. Peter, then, told her all about the fairies.

"You see, Wendy, when the first baby laughed for the first time, its laugh broke into a thousand pieces, and they all went skipping about, and that was the beginning of fairies. And so, there ought to be one fairy for every boy and girl." "What do you mean by ought to be? Isn't there a fairy for every one?" "No. Nowadays, children don't believe in fairies. And every time a child says, 'I don't believe in fairies,' somewhere, a fairy falls down dead." He was speaking thus, when he remembered that Tinker Bell was nowhere to be seen.

"Oh No! Where has she gone? Tinker, Tinker, where are you?" Peter called out.

Wendy's heart fluttered with a sudden thrill. "Peter, do you want to tell me that a fairy is present in this very room!" she cried.

"She was here just now," Peter said, a little impatiently. "You don't hear her, do you?"

They both listened. "The only sound I am able to hear is the tinkling of the bells," said Wendy.

"Well, that's Tink! It's the fairy language. I think I can hear her too."

They soon found that the sound came from the chest of drawers.

"Wendy," Peter whispered, "I think that I have shut Tinker Bell in the drawer!" They immediately opened the drawer and let Tinker Bell out. Tinker flew about the nursery screaming with fury. "I am very sorry, but how could I have known that you were in the drawer?" Peter said. Wendy was so surprised to see the fairy that she was not listening to their conversation.

"O Peter," she cried, "please ask her to stand still, let me see her!" "They hardly ever stand still," he said.

But for one moment, Wendy saw Tinker Bell resting on the cuckoo clock.

"O how lovely!" she cried, though Tink's face was still in anger.

"Tink," said Peter amiably, "this young lady says she wishes you were her fairy." Tinker Bell answered rudely. "What is she saying Peter?" Peter translated the fairy language for Wendy. "She says that you are an ugly girl, and she is my fairy." Peter tried to persuade Tink, "Tink, you can't be my fairy, I am a gentleman and you are a lady." Tink replied to this in some silly words and disappeared into the bathroom.

"Actually, she is quite a common fairy," Peter explained to Wendy.

"She is called Tinker Bell because she mends the pots and kettles; she's a tinker-tin worker." Wendy then posed Peter with some more questions. "With whom do you live mostly, these days?" "I live with the lost boys." "Who are they?" "They are the children who fall out of their prams, when their nurse is busy with other things. If they are not claimed in seven days, they are sent far away to the Neverland to settle expenses. I am the captain of the lost boys." "It must be real fun!"

"Yes," said cunning Peter, "but we are rather lonely. You see, we have no female companionship." "That means that there are no girls there." "Oh no, girls are too clever to fall out of their prams!" These words flattered Wendy. Peter Pan knew very well how to flatter girls. "You may give me a kiss," she told Peter happily, but just in time, she remembered that he didn't know what it was.

"Oh dear," said the nice Wendy, "I mean you can give me a thimble." And then Wendy kissed him. "Funny!" said Peter gravely. "Now shall I give you a kiss?" "If you wish to," said Wendy. So, they again exchanged thimbles. From that time onwards, they called a kiss, thimble and thimble, a kiss. Peter then told Wendy the reason for coming to the Darling's house. He often came to the nursery window to listen to the stories Mrs. Darling told them.

"You see, I don't know any stories. None of the lost boys knows any stories." "That is really bad," Wendy remarked. Suddenly, he remembered that he had to return to the lost boys. So, he rushed out of the window.

"Don't go, Peter," Wendy entreated, "I know lots of stories." Hearing these words, Peter came back to Wendy. "Wendy, can't you come with me and tell stories to other boys also?" he said eagerly. "Oh dear, I can't leave my mother. Besides, I can't fly," she said. "I'll teach you. And, Wendy, don't you want to see mermaids?" "Mermaids! With tails?" cried Wendy.

"Such long tails." "Oh," cried Wendy, "it would be great to see a mermaid!" Peter had become frightfully cunning now. "Wendy," he said, "you could take care of us by tucking us in at night and stitching clothes for us." Wendy couldn't resist such a big temptation.

"It's really fascinating!" she cried. "Peter, will you teach John and Michael to fly too?" "If you like," he said, indifferently. Wendy ran to wake John and Michael. They got up, rubbing their eyes. Wendy told her brothers all about Peter.

"Peter, can you really fly?" asked John.

Avoiding to be troubled by another set of questions, he flew around the room.

Now they all tried flying one by one. It was easy, but they always went down while flying instead of going up. Then Peter sprinkled some fairy dust on each of them, with the most superb results. "Now, just wiggle your shoulders this way," he said, "and let go." Soon all three children were flying across the room, though they didn't look as elegant as Peter. Up and down they went, and round and round.

It was just at this moment that Mr. and Mrs. Darling were hurrying towards the house. They would have made it on time, if the little stars in the sky had not played a trick. They would have reached the nursery in time had it not been for the little stars that were watching them. The stars blew the window open, and the smallest of the stars called out: "Run, Peter!" Peter at once knew that there was not a moment to lose.

"Come, it's time," he cried and soared high in the sky. He was followed by John, Michael, and Wendy. Mr. and Mrs. Darling and Nana were too late. The nursery was empty.

Chapter 4

The First Encounter

hen Peter had told Wendy the address of Neverland, he had said anything that came into his head.

At first, Peter's companions trusted him completely because for them it was delightful to fly. So happy they were that they wasted time circling round church spires. They had flown a great distance but had not reached Neverland. They had flown past the seas, the mountains and through the fluffy clouds. According to John's calculation, they had crossed two seas and were flying for three days. They were feeling sleepy and the moment they popped off, they started falling.

The dreadful thing was that Peter enjoyed all this. He thought this all funny! "There he goes again!" he would cry happily, as Michael suddenly dropped like a stone.

"Please save him, save him!" Wendy would scream with horror looking down at the cruel sea far below.

Peter would then dive through the air, and catch Michael just before he would strike the sea. But he always waited till the last moment, as he considered it as a game where the important thing was excitement. Peter, himself, could sleep in the air without falling, by merely lying on his back and floating. With such adventures, they drew near to Neverland. "Look, there it is," said Peter, suddenly. "Where, where?" the three

children said simultaneously and craned their necks, trying to get a look at it. "Where all the arrows are pointing," replied Peter. Indeed, there were about a million golden arrows of the sun, which were pointing out the island of Neverland. You see, the sun wanted them to be sure of their way before he bid the children goodnight and left them.

Wendy, John and Michael kept still in the air for a few minutes and looked at the island. They recognized it at once! It was not like something they had seen in their dreams, but like some friend to whom they were returning for their holidays.

However, the arrows of the sun left them with the sunset. The island was once again sunk in darkness. And suddenly, the children were filled with fear. There were no night lamps to cheer them on, and no Nana to comfort them.

Under the bright light of the sun, the three children were flying apart. But as the sun sank, they again huddled close to Peter. Now they were over the island of Neverland, flying so low that sometimes the leaves of the tree brushed their feet.

Nothing horrid was visible in the air, yet their progress had become slow and labored; it looked that as if they were flying against some hostile forces.

"They are trying their best to stop us from landing," Peter explained. "Who are they?" Wendy whispered, shuddering. But Peter remained silent. Tinker Bell had been asleep on his shoulder, but now he wakened her and sent her on in front. Peter kept floating in the air, listening carefully, with his hand on his ear. Having done these things, he asked John, "Would you like an adventure now or would you like to have your tea first?" Wendy was the first one to reply, she quickly said, "Tea first." Michael pressed her hand in gratitude. However, John was hesitant in answering.

"What kind of adventure is it?" he asked, cautiously. "There's a pirate asleep in the pampas just beneath us," Peter told him. "If you like, we'll go down and kill him." "I am not able to see him," John said after a long pause. "I do."

"Suppose," John, said, a little gruffly, "if he woke up?" "Were you thinking that I would be killing a man in his sleep?" Peter replied crossly. "I would wake him first, and then kill him." "How brave you are!" John exclaimed and then asked about the number of pirates present on the island that night.

"There are more than ever before," replied Peter. "Who is the captain now?" John inquired. "Hook," answered Peter, and his face became stern when he spoke his name.

"Hook!" Michael started crying when he heard the name. John gulped, for the children were aware of Hook's evil reputation. "What does he look like? Is he big?" asked John. "He is not as big as he was," replied Peter. "What do you mean?" John asked in a puzzled tone. "In our last fight, I cut off his right hand," Peter said triumphantly. "You did it?" exclaimed John, in disbelief.

"Yes, me," said Peter, gruffly. "Will he be able to fight now?" "Oh, he can!" "Then he must be fighting with his left hand?" asked Wendy. "He has an iron hook in place of his right hand and he claws with it." "Claws!" "I say, John," said Peter. "Every boy who joins my team promises me that if we ever meet Hook in an open fight, nobody except me will kill him." "I promise," John said, loyally.

They were feeling less creepy because Tink was flying with them, and in her light, they were able to see each other. Unfortunately, she could not fly as slowly as the children could, so she had to go round and round them in a circle, as in a halo. Wendy quite liked it, until Peter pointed out its drawbacks. "Tink tells me," Peter said, "that the pirates sighted us before the darkness came, and now, they are ready with the Long Tom." "Long Tom the big gun?" Michael asked

"Yes. And of course, if they see Tinker Bell's light, they are sure to shoot at us." "Then tell Tinker Bell," Wendy begged, "to put out her light." "She can't do that. The light leaves her only at the time of sleep, just like the stars." "If only one of us had a pocket," Peter wished, "we could have carried Tink in it." Then he had a brilliant idea. He cried, "John's hat! Tinker can very well hide there." Tink agreed to stay inside John's hat only if it was carried in his hand. At first, John carried it, but then Wendy took the hat, because John said it struck against his knee as he flew. Tink's light was completely hidden in John's black hat. They continued to fly in silence.

Then, all of a sudden, the air was charged by a tremendous crash. It was what Peter had feared; the pirates had fired Long Tom at them!

The roar of the fire echoed around the mountains. When at last, it died out John and Michael found that they were alone in the darkness. Peter had been flung far out into the sea, while Wendy and Tinker had been tossed heavenwards.

It would have been good if Wendy had dropped Tink out of the hat. Whether Tink had planned everything or it came instantly in her mind, I leave it on the readers to judge. She at once popped out of the hat and began to tempt Wendy to her destruction.

Tinker was not a bad fairy but she was jealous of Wendy. Wendy, who hadn't seen a fairy before, was so bewitched by little Tinker that she never doubted her intentions.

What Tinker said in her fairy language, Wendy couldn't understand but it sounded like, "Follow me, and all will be well."

Ignorant of Tinker Bell's intentions, Wendy followed her.

Chapter 5

Neverland-
The Island

Peter was brave enough to find his way back to the island. Sensing Peter's presence, the Neverland started blooming with life.

In Peter's absence, things were usually sluggish on the island. The fairies took an hour longer in the morning, the redskins fed heavily for six days. Even when the lost boys met the pirates, they merely bit their thumbs at each other. But when Peter came back on the island, everyone was once again active.

That evening, the lost boys were searching for Peter Pan, the pirates were out looking for the lost boys, the redskins were out looking for the pirates, and the beasts were out looking for the redskins. They were all moving around, but they did not meet each other because all were going at the same rate. On that day, the six lost boys, wearing skins of bears with daggers in their hands, were moving around the island in a file.

The first of them was Tootles, who was the humblest of all. Next one was Nibs, who was always merry and charming. Then was Slightly, the proudest among all the boys. The next was Curly who had the habit of landing in more than one or other mess. The last were the twins, who were always hazy about themselves, and did their best by staying close together in an apologetic sort of way.

Soon, the boys vanished in the darkness and the pirates came on their track. They

were singing the same dreadful song:

"A vast belay, yo-ho, heave to,
A-pirating we go,
And if we're parted by a shot
We're sure to meet below!"

There was never a more wicked and villainous-looking lot! The first to appear was the handsome Cecco, his great arms bare and pieces of eight in his ears as ornaments; he wrote his name in letters of blood on the back of his victims. Then there was Bill Jukes, whose entire body was tattooed. Then Cookson, who was said to be Black Murphy's brother. And gentleman Starkey had a very dainty method for killing, while Noodler's hands were fixed on backwards. Smee was an oddly friendly man and the only non-conformist in Hook's crew. Apart from them, the other noteworthy members of the pirate gang were Skylights, Mullins and Alf Mason.

The most terrible among these pirates was their captain, James Hook. Hook was a fierce looking man. He had long curly hair which gave a threatening expression to his face. His pale blue eyes shone like two red spots when he indulged in wicked pirate acts. He was a courageous man; the only thing he was afraid of was the sight of his own blood.

There was a holder always clamped between his teeth. This he had created himself; it enabled him to smoke two cigars at once. But undoubtedly, the grimmest part of him was his iron claw. Hook's terrible method of killing was to shoot forth his hook into his victim's body, then kick the body aside, and pass on. Even then, he did not take the cigars out from his mouth.

Such was the terrible man against whom Peter Pan was fighting.

James Hook hated Peter Pan and the lost boys. He made plans to kill Peter, who, during a battle, had cut off Hook's hand and thrown it to a passing crocodile. The crocodile had taken a liking to his flesh, and had been after Hook ever since. Hook was extremely fearful of the crocodile and ran away whenever it came near him.

On the trail of the pirates, walking noiselessly down the war-path, were the redskins. In front was the Great Big Little Panther, with so many scalps around his neck that it hindered his speed. At the end of the line was ferocious Tiger Lily. She was beautiful, cold at times and loving at others. All of them carried tomahawks and knives, and their naked bodies gleamed with paint and oil.

The redskins passed over the fallen twigs, without making the slightest noise. The only sound which could be heard from them was that of heavy breathing, as they had had a rather heavy meal that day and needed to walk it off.

As soon as the redskins disappeared, their place was taken by beasts: lions, tigers, bears, and other smaller savages. Every kind of beast, (particularly, all the man-eaters,) lived on this island. Due to hunger, their tongues were hanging out.

After the beasts, came a gigantic crocodile, looking for something.

The crocodile passed, but soon the lost boys appeared again, for the procession had to go on until one of the parties stopped or changed its pace.

The first to fall out of the moving circle were the lost boys. Tired, they flung themselves down on the grass.

"I wish Peter would come back," each one of the lost boys said. "I am not at all afraid of the pirates," Slightly boasted, "but I wish Peter would come back, and tell us whether he has heard anything more about Cinderella." Then the lost boys started talking about Cinderella. Tootles was confident that his mother must have resembled Cinderella. They spoke about mothers only in the absence of Peter Pan, because this topic was considered too silly and forbidden for any discussion.

While they talked, they heard a distant sound. You or I, not being wild things of the woods, could have heard nothing, but they heard it, and it was the grim song:

"Yo-ho, yo-ho,
The pirate life,
The flag o' skull and bones,
A merry hour, a hempen rope,
And hey for Davy Jones."

The lost boys disappeared at once, faster than the rabbits! But where did all of them go?

This query of yours will be answered by me. They were now comfortably settled in their home, which was under the ground.

But how did they reach home, as there was no entrance to be seen?

If you looked closely, you could see seven large trees. Each tree had a hole in its hollow trunk, which was sufficient to hold a boy. These were the seven entrances to the home under the ground. Hook had been searching for these entrances for a long time but all his searches had been futile.

As the pirates advanced, Starkey sighted Nibs disappearing through the wood. He took aim and was about to fire a shot, when an iron claw gripped his shoulder.

"Put back that pistol," said Hook threateningly, in his deep, dark voice. "It was one of those lost boys, why did you stop me?" said Starkey, filled with anger.

"Stupid! The sound of gun shot would have brought Tiger Lily's redskins here. Do you want to lose your skull? Just scatter around and look for the boys." The pirates started their search for the boys. Now, Captain Hook and Smee were alone.

What really happened, I don't know why, but suddenly Hook was overcome with a desire to confide to his faithful oarsman the story of his life. "Most of all," Hook said passionately, "I want the captain of the lost boys, Peter Pan. It was he who cut off my hand." He brandished the hook threateningly. "I've long waited to shake his hand with this. Oh, I'll rip him!"

"But," said Smee, "I have often heard you say that the hook is more useful than even a dozen hands, whether it's for combing the hair or for killing the enemy."

"Yes," agreed Hook, looking proudly at his iron hand for a while. "Peter flung my arm," he said, wincing, "to a crocodile, which happened to pass by." "Captain, I have often noticed that you are fearful of crocodiles," said Smee.

"I am not afraid of all crocodiles, but only of that one crocodile," Hook told him. He lowered his voice. "That crocodile liked my hand so much, Smee, that it has followed me ever since, from sea to sea and from land to land. Now, he wants to have the rest of me." "In a way," said Smee, "it's sort of a compliment." "I don't desire such compliments," Hook barked angrily. "I want that Peter Pan; it's because of him I am suffering." Now, Captain Hook sat down on a large mushroom.

"Smee," he said huskily, "it's my luck which has saved me from the clutches of the crocodile. That crocodile would have had me before this, but by a chance, it swallowed a clock which goes *tick, tick* inside it. So before it reaches me, I can hear the sound of the clock."

"But if some day," said Smee, "the clock runs down, then he will get you." Hook took a deep breath and said, "Yes, this fear haunts me day and night."

All of a sudden, Hook realized that since sitting down he had felt curiously warm. "Smee," he said, "this place is hot."

The next moment he jumped to his feet, crying, "Odds bobs, hammer and tongs, I'm burning!"

Then the two of them examined the mushroom on which he was sitting. To their surprise, it was extraordinarily large and tough. Then they tried to pull it up, and it came away at once in their hands, for it had no root!

Stranger still, smoke began to come up at once from the place where the mushroom had been.

"A chimney!" they both shouted with joy.

They had discovered the house of the lost boys. The lost boys used to stop the smoke from the chimney with a mushroom when their enemies were nearby. The voices of children could be heard from the chimney hole. The lost boys were feeling so safe in their hidden house that they were talking and chattering loudly and merrily. It was a good opportunity for the pirates; they listened carefully to the lost boys' chattering. They looked around them and noted the holes in the seven trees.

"Did you hear them say that Peter Pan is not at home?" Smee whispered. Hook nodded, but looking at his face one could sense that he was plotting something. At last, a blood-curdling smile lit up his dark face. Smee had been waiting for it.

"Let me know your plan, captain," he cried eagerly. "We will return to the ship, and cook a large, rich cake with green sugar on it. We will leave those sweet cakes on the shore of the Mermaids' Lagoon. These boys often play there with the mermaids. When they see the cake, I am sure they will not be able to resist. They will gobble it up, because, having no mother, they don't know how dangerous it is to eat rich, damp cake."

Hook then burst into a loud laughter, "Aha! They will die!" Smee listened with great admiration; he was more than happy with this idea. "It's the wickedest, prettiest policy ever I heard of!" he cried.

Filled with joy, they danced and sang:

"A vast, belay, when I appear,
By fear they're overtook;
Nought's left upon your bones
When you have shaken claws with Hook."

They had to leave their song and dance unfinished, as their attention was caught by another sound. As it came nearer, the sound was more distinct.

Tick, tick, tick, tick!

"The crocodile!" Hook gasped, and ran away, followed by Smee. Hook was not wrong in recognizing the sound. It was indeed the crocodile. It had passed the redskins, who were now on the trail of the other pirates. It followed only Hook. Once again, the lost boys came out of their underground house. But the dangers of the night were not yet over. Pursued by a pack of wolves, Nibs rushed to them for help. "Save me, save me!" cried Nibs, falling on the ground. The lost boys were terrified when they saw Nibs, followed by the pack of wolves.

"But what can we do, what can we do?" the lost boys said.

As always, their thoughts turned to Peter, who was clever in handling all these situations.

"What would Peter do?" they cried at the same time. Almost in the same breath, they cried, "Peter would look at them through his legs." Then, "Let us do exactly what Peter would do!" Together, they bent and looked through their legs at the wolves. It was the most successful way of defying wolves. When the boys advanced upon the beasts with this terrible attitude, the wolves dropped their tails and ran away. They all were happy at their success, but Nibs was preoccupied with some other thoughts.

"I have seen a *wonder-fuller* thing!" he cried, as all the boys gathered around him. "I saw a great white bird flying this way. As it flies, it moans, "Poor Wendy.""

"Poor Wendy?"

"I think you don't know that," said Slightly proudly, "there are birds called *Wendies*."

"See, here it comes!" cried Curly, pointing to little Wendy in the sky.

Wendy was now almost overhead, and they could hear her melancholic cry. But, more distinct was the shrill voice of Tinker Bell. The jealous fairy had now cast off all disguise of friendship, and was darting at poor Wendy from every direction, pinching savagely each time she touched.

"Hello, Tink," cried the lost boys, standing on the ground.

"I have an order for you from Peter; he wants you to shoot Wendy," Tink said. Peter's orders were never to be questioned. The lost boys ran to their trees to fetch bows and arrows. Tootles was the first one to return. Tinker Bell saw this as the right opportunity and said, "Quick, Tootles, quick; Peter will be so pleased."

Tootles excitedly fitted the arrow to his bow.

"Get out of the way Tink," he shouted.

Then he shot the arrow, which was on target.

Poor Wendy fell to the ground.

Chapter 6

A House for the Mother

hen the other boys came out armed from their trees, they saw Tootles standing like a conqueror over a body. It was Wendy's body.

"You are too late," he cried proudly. "I have shot Wendy. Peter will be so happy with me."

The boys crowded around Wendy. As they looked, a terrible silence fell upon the wood.

"Oh! This is not a bird," said Slightly in an anxious voice. "I think she is a lady."

"A lady?" said Tootles, and started trembling.

"Oh! And we have killed her," Nibs said, hoarsely.

"Now I can see things clearly," Curly said. "Peter was bringing a mother for us."

With these words Curly threw himself on the ground and started crying. Tootle's face

was white with sorrow, but he continued to mumble, "When ladies used to come in my dreams, I always said, 'Pretty mother, pretty mother.' But when she came to me at last, I shot her."

Thus they were lamenting, when Peter appeared in front of them. "Greetings, boys," he cried, cheerfully.

The boys remained silent; Peter was disappointed with this cold welcome.

He frowned for a second, and then spoke up again.

"I have great news! I have brought a mother for you all."

But this exciting news was also met with a complete silence.

"Have you not seen her?" asked Peter, looking troubled. "She flew this way, after the accident we met in the sky."

Tootles rose. "Peter," he said quietly, "we saw her, she is with us. I will show her to you."

The others were still standing before her, trying to hide the sight from Peter.

Tootles said to them, "Back, twins, let Peter see."

So they all stood back and let Peter see Wendy, and after he had looked for a few moments, he did not know what to do next.

He was mad with anger when he noticed the arrow, which had pierced her heart. He took it from Wendy's heart and questioned the members of his group.

"Whose arrow?" he demanded firmly.

"Peter, it is mine," said Tootles, crying.

Peter raised the arrow and was about to strike Tootles with it, when a hand rose to calm Peter.

It was Wendy's hand.

"The Wendy lady, see, her hand!" cried Nibs.

"She is alive!" Peter said.

Everyone was overjoyed!

Peter sat by Wendy; he found the button, which he had given to Wendy as a kiss, laying beside her. You remember she had put it on a chain that she wore round her neck.

"Look," said Peter, "the arrow struck against this. It has saved her life!"

Peter tried to talk to Wendy, but she couldn't answer any of his questions, being still in a frightful faint; but a wailing note could be heard from overhead.

"Listen to Tink," said Curly, "she is crying because Wendy has survived."

Then the lost boys narrated the story of Tinker Bell's mischief.

They had never seen Peter in such a temper.

"Listen, Tinker Bell," Peter cried, "you are not my friend any more. Go away from me for ever."

Tink was sorry for what she had done. She pleaded with Peter to forgive her. Tink again and again flew on to Peter's shoulder

but he brushed her off. It was only at Wendy's request that Peter relented sufficiently to say, "Well, not for ever, but for a whole week."

Do you think Tinker Bell was grateful to Wendy? Oh dear no, she never wanted to pinch her so much. Fairies indeed are strange, and Peter, who understood them best, often slapped them.

66

Peter's mind was occupied with another thought and that was how to deal with Wendy's injury.

"Let us carry her to the house," Curly suggested.

"No, no," Peter said, "you must not touch her. It would not be sufficiently respectful."

"But if she lies here, she will die," Tootles said, "she will die."

"Can't we build a little house around her?" Peter suggested.

This excellent plan was accepted by all.

"If only we could know," said one, "the kind of house she likes best."

"Wendy, can you please sing the kind of house you would like to have," Peter requested.

Without opening her eyes, Wendy began to sing:

"I wish I had a pretty house,

The littlest ever seen,
With funny little red walls
And roof of mossy green."

Listening to the song, the boys ran in to the woods. After some time, they returned with the branches sticky with red sap. They carpeted the ground with moss.

As they constructed the little house, they broke into song themselves:

"We've built the little walls and roof
And made a lovely door,
So tell us, mother Wendy,
What are you wanting more?"

To this, she answered greedily:

"Oh, really next I think I'll have
Gay windows all about,
With roses peeping in, you know,
And babies peeping out."

With a blow of their fists, they made windows. But from where were they to get the babies and roses? They pretended to grow the loveliest roses up the walls and forgot about the babies. Just then, when it looked like the house was complete, Peter noticed something:

"There's no knocker on the door," he said.

It was the sole of a shoe, which became an excellent knocker.

All the boys thought, "Now it's complete."

"No it isn't," said Peter. "There is no chimney!"

John's hat which was earlier used to carry Tinker Bell was now placed on the roof as a chimney. And immediately, smoke began to come out of the chimney!

Now the house looked quite complete. Nothing remained to be done but to knock.

"All should look their best," Peter warned them. "First impression is really important!"

Then Peter knocked the door of the house under the tree. The knock was answered by a pretty lady, who was none other than Wendy. All the boys whipped off their hats.

She looked surprised, and this was just how the boys had hoped she would look.

"Where am I?" she said.

Slightly was the first one to answer.

"Wendy lady," he said rapidly, "we built this house for you."

"Oh, aren't you pleased with it?" cried Nibs.

"It's a lovely house!" Wendy said, and the lost boys were happy to hear these words.

Then all the boys bent down on their knees, and holding out their arms, cried, "O Wendy lady, be our mother."

"Well," Wendy said, glowing, "I will try my best to be your mother, but I am only a little girl and have no real experience."

"That doesn't matter," said Peter.

"Then," she said, "Come inside at once, you naughty children; I am sure your feet are damp. I think I should tell you the story of Cinderella before putting you to bed."

So the lost boys went inside the house. I don't know how there was room for all of them, but you can squeeze very tight in the Neverland. This was one of the first joyous evenings of Wendy in the Neverland. Before long, she tucked up all the children in the great bed, in the underground home but she herself slept that night in the little house.

Wendy was their mother, and Peter had agreed to be their father. He kept watch outside with drawn sword, for the pirates could be heard carousing far away and the wolves were creeping around.

The little house looked cozy and safe in the darkness, with a bright light showing through its blinds, and the chimney smoking beautifully.

Chapter 7

Beneath the Earth

O nce Wendy was fine they all shifted to the underground house. The first thing that Peter did was to measure Wendy, John and Michael for hollow trees. This was important, for unless your tree fitted you, it was difficult to go up and down. Once you fitted, you could go up and down the tree quickly and efficiently. For the three Darling children, it was quite an adventure. They soon grew to love their cave home, especially Wendy.

The house consisted of one large room. In the floor of the room grew large mushrooms, of charming colors; they were used as stools. In the center of the room was the stump of a Never tree. The stump of the tree was used as a table by the lost boys. There was also an enormous fireplace in the room. Wendy stretched fiber strings across this, and hung her washing upon it. The bed

was let down at 6:30pm; the whole day it remained tilted against the wall. When it was let down, it filled nearly half the room. All the boys slept on the bed but since it was too crowded, Michael had to sleep in a small basket. There was a strict rule against turning around in the bed, until the signal was given. And when it was given, everyone turned at once!

There was a small nook in the wall, which was no larger than a bird cage. It was the home of Tinker Bell. It was shut off from the rest of the house by a tiny curtain, which Tink always kept drawn while dressing or undressing. There can be no woman who could possess a more beautiful dressing room and bed-chamber than Tink had. There was a beautiful couch, and she changed the bedspreads according to what fruit-blossom was in season. The little room also had a mirror, a chest of drawers, and the best of carpet and rugs. Tinker Bell lit her home with a pretty chandelier.

The whole day, Wendy was busy with the house work. You see, it was not easy to be the mother of eight children. Indeed, there were weeks when she couldn't find time to come above the ground.

The cooking, I can tell you, kept Wendy's nose to the pot, even if there was nothing in it! In Neverland, one never exactly knew whether there would be a real meal or just

make-believe meal; it all depended upon Peter's whim. But even make-believe was so real to Peter that during a meal of it, you could see him getting fatter!

When all the boys went to sleep, it was Wendy's favorite time for mending and sewing. There were always a lot of things for her to sew and darn. Whenever she sat down with the basketful of stockings, she would be tired of sewing the holes in the heel of each of them.

"Oh dear, I am sure I sometimes think the unmarried women are to be envied!" Wendy would fling up her arms and exclaim.

I don't know why, but her face beamed when she said these words.

You might wonder if Wendy missed her parents she had left behind. I am sorry to say that Wendy never missed her parents. She was sure that they would always keep the windows of the nursery open, so she could return whenever she wished. What did scare her sometimes was that John only vaguely remembered his parents, while Michael believed Wendy to be his real mother!

To make them remember about their old life, she asked them examination questions on their parents.

They were the most ordinary questions like:

1a. What was the color of Mother's eyes?

1b. Who was taller, Father or Mother?

1c. Was Mother blonde or brunette?

Answer all three questions if possible.

2. Write an essay of not less than 40 words on how I spent my last holidays, or the characters of Father and Mother compared. Or:

3a. Describe Mother's laugh;

3b. Describe Father's laugh;

3c. Describe Mother's party dress;

3d. Describe the kennel and its inmate.

All the little boys participated in this little game except Peter. Firstly, because

Peter disliked all mothers except Wendy, and secondly, he was the only boy on the island who could neither read nor write.

Adventures were part and parcel of daily life in Neverland. Like the night when the redskins attacked the house under the ground. Several of them got stuck in the hollow trees and had to be pulled out like corks.

How can we forget the cake trick of Captain Hook! Captain had prepared, in large quantity, sugar cakes and placed them in areas which were easily accessible to lost children. But Wendy always snatched them away from the hands of her children. In time, the cakes lost their moistness and became as hard as stone. They were finally used as missiles, and Hook fell over them in the dark.

No one could stay away from adventures in Neverland. Wendy too had a share of her adventures, which came in this way...

Chapter 8

Life or Death

everland had a lovely lagoon. The children spent the hot summer days swimming and floating in its clear blue waters.

Wendy had never seen mermaids before. When Wendy stole softly to the edge of the lagoon, she could see dozens of mermaids, especially on Marooners' Rock. Most of the mermaids came to relax here or for combing out their long silky hair. When the mermaids saw Wendy approaching them, they dived in the water, splashing Wendy with their tails, not by accident, but intentionally. It was impossible to catch the mermaids, for even if one managed to get hold of them, they slipped out easily for they were very, very slippery!

It was a beautiful day, and the lost boys were all on Marooners' Rock, sleeping in the sun. Finding it as an appropriate opportunity, Wendy was busy, stitching. While she was busy stitching, a change came over the lagoon and she was alarmed by a sudden shiver. The sun went away and shadows stole across the water, turning it cold. It grew extremely dark and Wendy was afraid; she could no longer thread her needle. The lagoon, that had always been such a laughing place, seemed frightening and unfriendly. Something as dark as night had sent that shiver through the sea, to say that it was coming.

Wendy was unable to understand; what was happening?

She recalled all the stories she had heard of Marooners' Rock. The rock was the favorite spot of the pirates for punishing their enemies. They used to leave their enemies on the rock for getting drowned. When the tide rose, the rock became submerged in water, thus drowning the men. Wendy was an inexperienced mother; she was recalling all this but she never thought to wake up the boys. She thought one must stick to the rule of resting for half an hour after the mid-day meal.

But luckily, there was a person who could sniff danger even in his sleep. He was none other than Peter Pan.

Peter sprang to his feet. With one warning cry, he roused the others. "Pirates!" he cried.

Hearing these words, others also leaped up from their sleep. A strange smile was

playing about Peter's face. While that smile was on his face, no one dared talk to him; all they could do was to obey. Then the order came, sharp and piercing.

"Dive!"

In a flash of a second, they dived in the water. The lagoon seemed deserted.

At that moment, a boat drew nearer to the rock. It was the pirate vessel, with three people in it – Smee, Starkey, and the third one was a captive, Tiger Lily, the daughter of the redskin chief.

The pirates had tied her ankles and hands. She knew that she was to be left on the rock to drown and die; her fate was sealed.

In the darkness, the two pirates did not see the rock till they crashed into it. The next moment the pirates landed the girl on the rock; she was too proud to offer a vain resistance.

Peter and Wendy were hiding near the rock. Wendy was crying as it was the first time that she was facing the pirates. Peter decided to save Tiger Lily. An easy way to save Tiger Lily would have been to wait until the pirates had left. But Peter was not that sort of boy and never chose the easy way.

Instead, he imitated the voice of Hook.

"What are you doing, you lubbers!" he called.

It was a marvelous imitation.

"The captain!" said the pirates, looking at each other in surprise.

"We are leaving Tiger Lily on the rock," Smee called out.

"Set her free," was the surprising answer.

"But, captain..."

"Do as I order, at once," said the voice, "or I'll sink my hook in you."

"Ay, ay," Smee said, and he cut Tiger Lily's cords. At once, like a fish, she slid between Starkey's legs and into the water.

Wendy was impressed by Peter's cleverness. But she also knew that he would be thrilled and would praise himself. So, at once her hand went out to cover Peter's mouth.

Suddenly, the lagoon rang up with, "Boat ahoy!" This time it was Hook himself and not Peter Pan.

Wendy now understood that the real Hook was also in the water. He swam towards his companions, guided by the lamp light. Starkey and Smee were curious to know the reason for their captain's coming. Hook sat down, with his head on the hook, in a position of profound melancholy.

"Captain, is everything well?" they asked apprehensively, but he answered with a heavy moan.

"He sighs," said Smee.

"He sighs again," said Starkey.

"And yet he sighs a third time," said Smee.

At last, Hook spoke passionately, "The game is up! The lost boys have at last found a mother."

Wendy, who was hearing all this conversation, swelled with pride.

"O evil day!" cried Starkey.

"What's a mother?" asked the ignorant Smee.

Wendy was so shocked to hear this, she exclaimed, "He doesn't know!" She felt like going to Smee and explaining all about a mother.

Just in time, Peter pulled her into the water, for Hook had started up, crying, "What was that?"

"I didn't hear anything," said Starkey, shining the lamp over the waters.

As they were looking over the waters, their eyes were caught by a strange sight. It was a nest floating on the lagoon, and the Never bird was sitting on it.

"Look," said Hook, ""that is a mother. What a lesson! The nest must have fallen into the water, but the mother didn't desert her eggs."

Smee was impressed by this sight; he kept on gazing at the bird and its nest. But the suspicious Starkey said, "Perhaps she is staying here to help Peter."

Hook winced.

"Ay," he said, "that is the fear that troubles me."

"Captain," said Smee, enthusiastically, "can't we kidnap the mother of the lost boys and make her our mother?"

"It is a strong plan," replied Hook. "We will kidnap the children and carry them to the boat. Then, we will make the boys walk the plank, and Wendy will be our mother."

Hearing this, once more, Wendy forgot herself.

"Never!" she cried.

"What was that? Is someone there?"

Again, they looked over the water with the help of their lamp. But they could see nothing. They concluded that it must be a leaf in the wind.

"Do you agree with the plan, my bullies?" asked Hook.

"We promise to execute this plan," they both said.

"And there is my hook. Swear," Hook said.

They all swore, and then suddenly looking at the rock, Hook remembered Tiger Lily.

"Where is the daughter of the redskin?" he demanded, unexpectedly.

Smee and Starkey thought that the captain was joking with them.

"That is all right, captain," Smee, answered haughtily, "how can we defy your orders? We let her go."

"*Let her go? On my orders!*" cried Hook.

"You called over the water to us to let her go," said Starkey.

"Brimstone and gall," thundered Hook, "what is happening here?"

Hook's face had gone red with anger.

"Friends," he cried, *"I never gave such an order!"*

"Something strange is going on here," Smee said, and they all looked around restlessly. Hook raised his voice again, but it was shaky this time.

"Spirit that haunts this dark lagoon tonight," he cried, "do you hear me?"

Now, how could have Peter remained quiet. He immediately answered in Hook's voice:

"Odds, bobs, hammer and tongs, I hear you."

At that moment, Hook did not even turn a shade pale, but Smee and Starkey clung to each other in terror.

"Who are you, voice? Speak!" Hook asked.

"I am James Hook," replied the voice, "captain of the *Jolly Roger.*"

"Why are you speaking lies? You are not; you are not," Hook cried gruffly.

"Brimstone and gall," the voice retorted, "if you say that again, you will not find yourself alive."

Hook tried another method of questioning the voice.

"If you are Hook," he said meekly, "then tell me, who am I?"

"A codfish," replied the voice, "just a codfish."

"A codfish!" Hook repeated. At this moment, he saw his men draw back from him.

"Were we governed by a codfish all this time?" they muttered. "It is shameful."

His own followers were snapping at him now! But, though he had become a tragic figure, Hook scarcely paid attention to them. Suddenly, he was tempted to try the guessing game with the voice.

"Hook," the captain called to the voice, "do you have another voice?"

Peter was unable to resist another game with Hook, therefore he answered unthinkingly in his own voice, "I have."

"And, do you have another name?"

"Ay, ay."

"Is it a Vegetable?" asked Hook.

"No."

"Then, is it a Mineral?"

"No."

"Man?"

"No!" This time the answer rang out scornfully.

"You are a boy then?"

"Yes."

"Are you an ordinary boy?"

"No!"

"Then a wonderful boy?"

To Wendy's surprise, this time Peter answered in affirmation, "Yes."

"Are you in England?"

"No."

"Are you here?"

"Yes."

By now, Hook was completely perplexed.

"You ask him some questions," he said to his fellows.

Smee thought for a moment.

"I can't think of any thing to ask," he said apologetically.

"Can't guess, can't guess!" crowed Peter, cheerfully. "So you give it up or want to try?"

"Yes, yes, we give it up. Reveal yourself," the pirates answered eagerly.

"Well, then, I will tell you," he cried. "I am Peter Pan."

"Peter Pan!" Hook cried; he was again himself and ready to kill. Smee and Starkey were his faithful followers.

"We will not leave him this time," Hook shouted. "Into the water. Smee! Starkey, mind the boat, I want him dead or alive!"

He jumped overboard as he spoke, and at that same time was heard the enthusiastic voice of Peter.

"Are you ready, boys?"

"Ay, ay," came the answer from the lost boys, hidden in various parts of the lagoon.

The fight was short and sharp. Here and there, a head bobbed up in the water, and there was a flash of steel followed by a cry or a whoop. Soon, Starkey and Smee swam away, deserting their captain.

What was Peter doing all this time?

He was confronting Hook, the bigger fish.

Hook rose to the rock to breathe, and at that same moment, Peter scaled it on the opposite side. The rock was very slippery, and they had to crawl rather than climb. Neither knew that the other was coming.

Each feeling for a grip met the other's arm, and in surprise, they raised their heads. Their faces were almost touching.

Peter snatched the knife from Hook's belt and was about to drive it in him, when he realized that he was standing higher up on the rock than his enemy was. Peter believed in fair fight, so, he gave a hand to Hook to help him, but have you heard of any pirate being an honest man? Peter was trying to help Hook; in return, Hook bit him.

It was not the pain of the bite, but its unfairness, which stunned Peter. It made him quite helpless. Twice the iron hand clawed him, but he only stared in horror.

A few seconds later, the lost boys noticed Hook swimming wildly towards the ship. He looked terrified, as he was being chased by a crocodile.

On ordinary occasions, the boys would have cheered the crocodile but today they were uneasy, for they couldn't see Peter and

Wendy anywhere. Thus, they were hunting the lagoon for them, calling them by name. They found the vessel and went home in it, shouting, "Peter, Wendy" as they went. But they received no answer.

When their voices died away, a cold silence enveloped the lagoon.

And then, there arose a feeble cry.

"Help, help!"

Two small figures were beating against the rock; the girl had fainted and lay on the boy's arm. It was Wendy with Peter. It took him a lot of effort, to pull her up the rock. Even as he too fainted, he saw that the water was rising and knew that they would soon be drowned. But he didn't have the strength to do anything.

As they were lying side by side on the rock, a mermaid caught Wendy by the feet, and started pulling her softly into the water. Peter, feeling her slip from him, woke with a start, and was just in time to draw her back. Wendy had regained consciousness and Peter thought it best to tell the truth.

"We are on the rock, Wendy," he said. "Soon the water will be over it, and we will be drowned."

"Shall we swim or fly, Peter?" asked Wendy.

"Do you think you have the strength to fly as far as the island, without my help?"

She had to admit that she was too tired.

"I am helpless Wendy. Hook has wounded me. I can neither fly nor swim."

"Do you mean we will be drowned?"

"Look how the water is rising."

They prepared themselves for the worse. They put their hands over their eyes to shut out the sight of water. As they sat, something brushed against Peter as light as a kiss. It was the tail of a kite, which Michael had made some days ago. It had torn itself from Michael's hand and floated away.

The next moment, Peter seized its tail, and pulled the kite towards him.

"If it can lift Michael off the ground," he cried, "why shouldn't it lift you?"

"Can't it carry both of us?" asked Wendy.

"It can't lift two; Michael and Curly had tried that."

Then, quickly, he tied the tail of the kite round Wendy. Wendy clung to Peter, refusing to go without him. But Peter didn't listen to her pleas. He quickly said, "Goodbye, Wendy," and pushed her from the rock. Soon, Wendy was out of his sight.

Peter was now alone on the lagoon, waiting for the rock to be submerged. He was thinking, "To die will be an awfully big adventure."

Chapter 9

The 'NEST' of the Never Bird

T he last sound Peter heard before he was quite alone, were the mermaids retiring one by one to their bedchambers under the sea. The water was rising steadily; it was now touching Peter's feet. At this moment, Peter's eyes were caught by a piece of paper drifting on the surface of the water. What Peter thought was a piece of paper, was the Never bird making desperate efforts to reach Peter on the nest.

She had come to save him, to give him her nest, though her eggs were still in it.

"I -- want -- you -- to -- get -- into -- the -- nest," the bird called, speaking as slowly and clearly as possible, "and -- then -- you -- can -- drift -- ashore, but -- I -- am -- too - - tired -- to -- bring -- it -- any -- nearer

-- so -- you -- must -- try -- to -- swim -- to -- it."

Peter was actually not able to hear what the Never bird was saying.

"What are you quacking about?" Peter asked. "Why don't you let the nest flow as usual?"

"I -- want -- you --," the bird said, and repeated the purpose of drifting the nest towards Peter.

Peter tried again to understand what it was saying.

"What -- are -- you -- quacking -- about?" and so on.

Never birds are short tempered; when the bird realized that Peter was unable to understand her, she became angry.

"You dunderheaded little jay!" she screamed. "Why don't you do as I tell you?"

Peter felt that the Never bird was insulting him, so he too replied hotly:

"So are you!"

Then rather curiously, they both snapped out the same remark:

"Shut up!"

"Shut up!"

In spite of all this, the Never bird was determined to save him. With one last mighty effort, she propelled the nest against the rock. Then she flew up in the air, to make Peter understand her intentions of saving him, not her eggs.

At last, Peter understood. He clutched the nest and waved his thanks to the bird as she fluttered overhead. Two large eggs were lying in the nest; Peter lifted them up and reflected. The bird covered her face with her wings, so as not to see the end of her two precious eggs. But she could not help peeping between the feathers.

Intelligent Peter found a beautiful solution to the problem. He spotted Starkey's hat lying on the rock, put the eggs in to the hat and set it afloat.

The Never bird screamed in admiration, when she saw what Peter was up to. At that moment, the bird fluttered down upon the hat and once more sat comfortably on her eggs. Then Peter got into the nest, and hung up his shirt for a sail. The Never bird drifted in one direction, and Peter was borne off in another, both happy.

When Peter reached the shore, he left the nest in such a place, where the bird would easily find it. But the Never bird liked the hat so much that it abandoned its nest forever. From that day on, Starkey often came to the shore of the lagoon, and with many bitter feelings watched the Never bird sitting on his hat.

Peter reached his underground home almost as soon as Wendy, who had arrived there by kite. Every one of them had some adventure to tell, but the biggest adventure was that they were several hours late for bed. Wendy, angry at the lateness of bedtime, cried, "To bed, to bed," in a voice that had to be obeyed.

Chapter 10

The Happy Home

The act of saving Tiger Lily from the pirates made the redskins and the lost boys very good friends. Tiger lily and her companions were so grateful to Peter that they would do anything for him.

Night and day the redskins kept watch over the under ground home of the lost boys, awaiting the big attack by the pirates.

Now we come to the evening that was to be known among them as the 'Night of Nights', because of its adventures and their outcome. The redskins were at their posts, while the children were having their evening meal in the underground house. All were there except Peter, who had gone out somewhere.

Like all children, the lost boys also troubled their mother. After their meal, the boys started complaining to their mother about each other. Wendy told them to clear away, and sat down with her stitching work.

"Wendy," scolded Michael, "I'm too big for a cradle."

"I can't leave the cradle empty and you know that there is not enough space on the bed," she said almost sharply. "You are the smallest among all children. A cradle is such a nice homely thing to have about a house."

The children danced around Wendy in a circle, while she remained busy sewing.

Suddenly, there was a step above, and

Wendy, you may be sure, was the first to recognize it.

"Children, I hear your father's step. He would like you to meet him at the door." Immediately the children surrounded him happily.

Peter had brought nuts for the boys, and pretty berries for Wendy to put in her hair.

"Peter, you will spoil them, you know," Wendy said.

"Ah, mother," said Peter, hanging his gun on the wall.

One of the twins came to Peter and said "Father, we would like to dance."

"Dance away, my little man," said Peter, who was very happy that day.

"But we want you to dance with us."

Peter was the best dancer among all the boys but he pretended that he didn't know how to dance.

"Me! My old bones would rattle!"

"Mummy too will dance with us."

"What?" cried Wendy. "How can the mother of so many children dance?"

But children are not so easily persuaded; the children pleaded hard and at last, Peter and Wendy gave in.

They sang and danced in their night-gowns.

The dance was funny; it was more of a pillow fight than a dance. When it was finished, the pillows insisted on one round more!

At last, they all got in to the bed for Wendy's good night story, the story which they loved the most. But this story was hated by Peter. Usually, when Wendy began to tell this story he left the room, but tonight he remained on his stool; let's see what happened.

Chapter 11

Wendy Tells a Story

isten boys!" said Wendy, starting the story, with Michael at her feet and seven boys in the bed.

"Once upon a time, there was a gentleman..."

"I'd rather he had been a lady," Curly said.

"I wish he had been a rat," added Nibs.

"Quiet," their mother ordered them.

"There was a lady also and..."

"Oh, mummy," cried the first twin, "I hope that the lady is not dead?"

"Oh no!", replied Wendy.

"I am so happy she isn't dead," said Tootles.

"Are you glad, John?"

"Of course I am."

"Are you glad, Nibs?"

"Yes, too glad."

"Are you glad, Twins?"

"We are glad."

"Oh dear," sighed Wendy.

"Make less noise," Peter called out, determined that Wendy should have a chance to complete her story, however beastly a story it might be in his opinion.

"The gentleman's name," Wendy continued, "was Mr. Darling, and the woman's name was Mrs. Darling."

"I knew them," John said, to tease the others.

"I think I knew them too," said Michael, rather doubtfully.

"They had three children," continued Wendy. "The children had a loving nurse called Nana. One day, Mr. Darling was angry with her and chained her up in the yard, and all the children flew away."

"It's a very good story," cried Nibs.

"They flew away to Neverland where the lost boys lived," Wendy continued. "Oh mother!" cried Tootles, "was the name of one of the lost children Tootles?"

"Yes, it was."

"I am part of the story. Hurrah! I am in the story, Nibs."

"Hush...... Now I want you to think about how Mr. and Mrs. Darling felt after their children had flown away."

"Oo!" they all moaned.

"Think of the empty beds!"

"Oo!"

"It's very sad," the first twin said, cheerfully.

Wendy was now on that part of the story which Peter hated a lot.

"You see," Wendy, said, contentedly, "the heroine of the story was sure that the mother would always leave the window open for her children to fly back. So, they stayed in Neverland for years and had a lovely time."

"Did they ever go back?" asked Tootles.

"Yes, one day they did return. They flew to their mummy and daddy through the open window, and everyone was so happy once again."

When Wendy finished the story, Peter uttered a hollow groan.

"What is it, Peter?" Wendy cried, running to him, thinking he was ill.

"Wendy, you are wrong about mothers."

All the boys gathered around Peter who, looking a bit agitated, revealed the secret that he had been concealing.

"Long ago," he said, "I used to think like you; I believed that my mother would always keep the window open for me, so I stayed away for moons and moons, and then flew back. But the window was closed, and I saw another little boy sleeping in my bed."

All the boys were terrified to hear this.

"Wendy, let us go home," cried John and Michael together.

"Yes," she said, clutching them.

"We hope you are not leaving us tonight?" asked the lost boys, puzzled.

"At once," Wendy replied firmly, for the horrible thought had passed her mind, 'Perhaps mother is in half-mourning by this time.'

This fear made her forget to think what Peter might be feeling. She said to him rather sharply, "Peter, will you make the necessary arrangements for our return?"

"If you wish so," he replied, rather coldly. "Tinker Bell will take you across the sea."

But of course, Peter cared a lot for Wendy but he was full of scorn for grown-ups who, as usual, were spoiling everything.

The lost boys were looking sadly at Wendy who, along with John and Michael were preparing for the journey. The boys were sad because not only would they be losing their mother; they also felt that she was going off to something nice to which they had not been invited.

Looking at their unhappy faces, Wendy's heart melted.

"Dear boys," she said, "if you will come with me, I am sure that my parents will also adopt you."

At once, the boys jumped with joy.

"Peter, can we go?" they all cried imploringly.

They never thought that Peter might not wish to accompany them.

"All right," Peter replied with a bitter smile.

After getting Peter's approval, the boys rushed to pack up their things. "Now, Peter," Wendy said, thinking that she had made everything fine, "I think you should have your medicine before we leave."

Wendy's favorite job was to give medicine to everyone. Of course, it was only water, but it was out of a bottle, and she always shook the bottle and counted the drops, which gave it a certain medicinal quality. She was about to give certain drops of medicine to Peter, when she saw a look on his face that made her heart sink.

"Pack your things, Peter," she cried, shaking.

"No," he answered, pretending to be indifferent to what was happening.

"I am not going with you, Wendy."

"Yes, you are, Peter."

"No."

"To find your mother," she tried to persuade.

"No, no," Peter said decisively, "perhaps she would say I am old now, and I always wanted to be a little boy and have fun."

"But, Peter…"

"No."

This news had to be told to the other boys, so, Wendy cried, "Peter isn't coming."

When the boys heard that Peter was not coming with them, they gazed blankly at each other.

When Peter saw the sorrowful look on their faces, he cried, "No fuss, no blubbering; good-bye Wendy." Peter held out his hand cheerily, quite as if they must leave him now, for he had something important to do.

This time, there was no indication that he would prefer a thimble, so Wendy had to take his hand.

"Peter, I hope you will remember changing your flannels?" she said, lingering over him. She was always so particular about their flannels.

"Yes."

"And you will take your medicine on time?"

"Yes."

This was followed by an awkward silence. Peter was not the kind of person who breaks down before other people.

"Are you ready, Tinker Bell, to show them the way home?" he called out.

"Ay, ay," answered Tink.

"Then lead the way."

Tink flew up in to the sky, but no one followed her. It was the moment chosen by the pirates to attack the redskins. On the ground, where all had been so still, the air was charged with shrieks and the clash of steel.

In the underground house, there was pin drop silence. Wendy fell on her knees, with her arms extending towards Peter. All arms were extended to him; all were insisting him mutely not to leave them. As for Peter, he got hold of his sword and was ready for the battle.

Chapter 12

The Enemy Attacks

T he attack of the pirates was a complete surprise. The brave Tiger Lily and her stoutest warriors suddenly saw the treacherous pirates bearing down upon them. The poor redskins had no chance of winning at all.

Hook was jubilant over the fact that his gang had overpowered the redskins. But this happiness was not reflected on his face. He had not come to fight against the redskins;

they were only the bees to be smoked so that he should get at the honey. His real enemy was Peter Pan, and his search had bought him here.

Captain Hook was agitated more by Peter's impudence than by his courage or appearance. But the big question that Hook now faced was how to reach the underground house, through the holes in the trees.

Let us now get back to the lost boys. What were they doing in the meantime?

All their efforts had failed to convince Peter Pan. The uproar on the ground between the redskins and the pirates had ceased as suddenly as it had erupted.

But the little boys knew that in the passing it had determined their fate.

"Which side has won?"

The pirates were listening to all this conversation, standing with their ears pressed to the mouth of the trees. They heard the question put by the boy and waited for Peter's answer.

"If the redskins have won," he said, "they will beat the tom-tom; it is always their sign of victory."

Smee had found the tom-tom from somewhere. Hook signaled to him to beat the tom-tom. At once, Smee understood the intentions of his captain. Twice Smee beat upon the instrument, and then stopped to listen, gleefully.

"It's the tom-tom," the criminals heard Peter cry; "an Indian victory!"

The lost children jumped with happiness, and immediately, they repeated their good-byes to Peter.

The pirates couldn't understand the reason for these good-byes, but they were delighted by the fact that their enemy would soon be coming out from their hiding. Rapidly, Hook issued his orders - one man to each tree, and the others to arrange themselves in a line two yards apart.

The first to emerge from his tree was Curly. He rose out of it into the arms of Cecco, who flung him to Smee, who flung him to Starkey, who flung him to Bill Jukes, who flung him to Noodler, and so he was tossed from one person to another till he fell at the feet of Captain Hook.

All the boys were plucked from their trees in the same ruthless manner. However, Wendy was treated in a different manner. With politeness, Hook raised his hat and offered her his arm. Then, he escorted her to the spot where the others were kept. Wendy was just a little girl; she was easily taken by the manners that Hook displayed before her, therefore she didn't cry out.

The boys were then tied to prevent their flying away, and then doubled up with their knees close to their ears. All was going according to the plan, until Slightly's turn came. The pirates failed in tying him up, for each time, there were no ends left to tie the knot. Furious, the pirates kicked Slightly, until Hook told them to stop. He knew what the problem was.

Hook's lip was curled up with a wicked smile. He had found out the cause behind this problem. And it was this: Slightly used to drink huge amounts of water when he was hot. Because of this, his body swelled up. And then, instead of reducing his weight so that he could fit into the passageway of his tree, he had increased the size of the passageway to accommodate his body!

Now that Hook knew the secret, his mind was ready to execute another treacherous plan. He immediately ordered his comrades to take the captives to the ship but he didn't accompany them, he stayed back, alone.

When all had left, the first thing Hook did was to tiptoe to Slightly's tree, which was wide enough to provide him with a passage. For a long time, he stood listening for any sound. But no sound could be heard; all was as silent below as above.

Was Peter asleep, or did he stand waiting at the foot of Slightly's tree, with his dagger in his hand?

Hook took courage; first, he slipped softly to the ground and stepped into the tree. He let himself go into the unknown. He arrived safely at the foot of the shaft and stood still. He was in the underground house; his eyes took some time to get accustomed to the dim light in the room. He saw various objects in the home but the one whom his eyes were seeking was lying on the great bed.

Peter Pan lay on the bed, fast asleep, unaware of the tragedy which had befallen his children.

After Wendy and the lost boys left him with their last good-bye, Peter had continued to play gaily on his pipes. Then he decided not to take his medicine, just to trouble Wendy. No doubt, he was trying to prove that he didn't care for anyone. Later, he sprawled on the bed outside the coverlet, and fell asleep. He had fallen at once into a deep sleep with one arm dropping over the edge of the bed, one leg arched, and the unfinished part of his laugh stranded on his mouth.

Hook was standing silently at the foot of the tree, looking across the chamber at his defenseless enemy. Suddenly, his eye caught sight of Peter's medicine kept on a shelf within easy reach. Hook always carried with him a dreadful drug, which was the deadliest poison ever found. Hook added five drops of this poison to Peter's medicine. Then, he took a last look at his victim and wormed his way with difficulty up the tree.

Peter continued to sleep. It must have been not less than ten o'clock by the crocodile's clock, when he was awakened by a soft tapping on the door of his tree.

"Who is that?"

The visitor replied, in a lovely bell-like voice.

"Let me in, Peter."

Peter rushed to open the door. It was Tink knocking. She flew in excitedly, her face flushed.

"What is it?"

"Oh, you don't know what has happened?" she cried, informing Peter about the kidnap of the lost boys and Wendy.

"I'll rescue her!" he cried, leaping at his weapons.

As he leapt out for his weapons, he thought of doing something to please Wendy. Then, he remembered Wendy asking him to have his medicine daily. Peter took the poisoned medicine bottle from the shelf.

"No!" shrieked Tinker Bell, who had heard Hook mutter about the evil deed as he sped through the forest.

"Why should I not drink the medicine?"

"It is poisoncd."

"Poisoned? Who would poison it?"

"James Hook."

"Don't be silly. How would Hook come down here?"

Tinker Bell had no answer to this question, as she did not know the dark secret of Slightly's tree. Meanwhile, Peter raised the cup to his lips. There was no time left for explaining things; immediately, Tinker Bell got between his lips and the draught, and drank the whole liquid.

"Tink, how dare you drink my medicine?" cried Peter.

Tinker Bell was not in any condition to answer; she was rolling in the air. "What has happened to you?" cried Peter, suddenly afraid.

"It was poisoned, Peter," she whispered; "and now I am going to die."

"O Tink, did you drink it to save me?"

"Yes."

"But why did you do it, Tink?"

Her wings would scarcely carry her now, but in reply to Peter's question, Tink landed on his shoulder and gave his nose a loving bite. She whispered in his ear, "You silly boy," and then, stumbling to her chamber, she lay down on the bed.

Peter was distressed to see Tinker Bell's critical condition. He sat beside her and was filled with sorrow to see that the light which glowed around the little fairy was slowly fading. Peter knew that if the light went out, his little fairy would be gone.

Peter was not able to restrain his tears. When Tink saw Peter crying, she liked his tears so much that she put out her beautiful finger and let them run over it. Tinker Bell was trying to say something to him, but her voice was so low that Peter could not make out what she said.

It took him a few minutes to understand that she was saying that she could get well again if children believed in fairies.

At once, Peter flung out his arms. He addressed all children, all the little boys and girls in the world: "If you believe in fairies, clap your hands; don't let Tink die."

There was silence all around.

Does not even one single child believe in fairies?

Then, all of a sudden, the sound of millions of little hands clapping filled the air.

Thus, Tink was saved. First, her voice grew strong, then she popped out of bed, and finally, she was flashing around the room, merrier than ever.

The next task which occupied Peter's mind was to save Wendy.

"And now we have to rescue Wendy!" cried Peter

It was night when Peter, belted with weapons, came out of his tree. He had set out on a dangerous journey without any clue of the direction. He was not sure if the children had been taken to the pirate ship. A light snow fall had erased all the footmarks. Peter had taught the children something of the forest wisdom that he had himself learned from Tiger Lily and Tinker Bell. And he was sure of the fact that in time of trouble the children would not forget to use it. For example, Slightly, if he had an opportunity, would cut a mark in the trees. Curly would drop seeds, and Wendy would leave her handkerchief at some important place. But to trace these marks, he had to wait for the morning.

But Peter could not wait till morning.

There was not a single living being that could be seen or heard of in the darkness of night. Yet, Peter knew well that sudden death might be at the next tree, or stalking him from behind. Not afraid of anything, he moved with a finger on his lips and a dagger, ready to strike.

At this moment, Peter took a terrible oath, "Hook or me this time."

Chapter 13

The Trick of Tick-Tick

olly Roger, the pirate ship, lay low in the water. The ship had been witness to many foul and bloody deeds committed by the pirates, all over the years.

The ship was wrapped in the blanket of night, through which no sound could have reached the shore. A few of the pirates leant over the ship's bulwarks; others drooped by barrels over games of dice and cards.

But their Captain Hook was not participating in any of these activities; rather, he was walking alone on the deck. Although it should have been his hour of victory, as Peter had been removed from his path forever and all the lost boys and their mother were his captives, yet there was no joy in his steps. He looked greatly dejected.

Hook was terribly alone; it was not the first time he was feeling so. Whenever he was surrounded by his own fellow men, he felt lonely. It sounds absurd but he felt that his men were socially inferior to him. Hook had been at a famous public school; and its traditions still clung to him like garments.

Meanwhile, the pirates, thinking that the captain was absorbed in his own thoughts, broke into a drunken dance. This brought Hook to his feet at once, all traces of human weakness gone, as if a bucket of water had passed over him.

"*Quiet*, you wild fellows," he cried, "or I'll throw you in the sea!"

The pirates, at once, obeyed the order of their captain and there prevailed a drop dead silence on the ship.

"Are all the children chained, so that they cannot fly away?"

"Ay, ay."

"Then bring them here."

The wretched prisoners were dragged out and placed in a line in front of Hook. Wendy was exempted from this treatment.

"Now," Hook said quickly, "six of you will walk the plank tonight, but I have space for two cabin boys. Which of you will be them?"

"Don't irritate Hook unnecessarily," was Wendy's instruction to her children. So, Tootles stepped forward and explained wisely, "Sir, you see, my mother would not like me becoming a pirate. Would your mother like it, Slightly?"

Tootles winked at Slightly, who said mournfully, "I don't think so."

"Would your mother like you to be a pirate, Twin?"

"I don't think so," replied the first twin, who was as clever as the others were.

"Nibs, would—"

"Shut up," roared Hook.

"You, boy," Hook said, pointing to John, "did you never desire to be a pirate?"

John was terrified by the fact that Hook had chosen him over all the other boys.

"I once thought of calling myself Red-handed Jack," he said, shyly.

"A nice name; if you join us, we will call you by that name," declared Hook.

"What would you call me if I join?" Michael asked.

"Black-beards Joe."

The name impressed Michael.

"What do you think, John?" asked Hook.

"Shall we still be respectful subjects of the King?" John inquired.

Hook answered, "You would have to swear, "Down with the King.""

Perhaps John had not behaved very well so far, but he shone out now.

"I refuse to take any such oath," he cried, and knocked down the barrel in front of Hook.

"I refuse too," cried Michael.

"Rule Britannia!" squeaked Curly.

Hook growled, "Your fate is sealed, bring up their mother. Get the plank ready."

The lost boys got afraid when they saw Jukes and Cecco preparing the plank but they tried to look brave when Wendy was brought in front of Hook.

"So, mother," said Hook, "shortly you will see your children walk the plank."

"Are they to die?" asked Wendy, with a look of frightful contempt. Hook didn't expect that Wendy would take the news in such a way.

"They are," he growled.

"Silence all," he then called out gloatingly; "so, what will be the last words of a mother for her children?"

At this moment, Wendy looked very majestic.

"Dear boys, these are my last words," she said firmly. "I feel it is my duty to convey to you the message of your real mothers, and it is this: 'we hope our sons will die like English gentlemen.'

The pirates were also impressed by this speech. Tootles cried out, "I am going to do what my mother hopes."

"What will you do, Nibs?"

"What my mother hopes."

"What will you do, Twin?"

"What my mother hopes. John, what are...?"

This was interrupted by Hook's growling, "Tie her up!"

Following the captain's order, Smee tied Wendy to the mast.

"See here, honey," he whispered, "I'll save you if you promise to be my mother."

Wendy was determined not to make any such promise.

"I would rather have no children at all," she said disdainfully.

It was sad to know that not one boy was looking at her as Smee tied her to the mast; the eyes of all were on the plank: that last little walk they were about to take. They were no longer able to hope that they would walk it manfully, for the capacity to think had gone from them; they could only stare and shiver.

Hook was happy to see that his revenge was fulfilled. He smiled as he saw the lost boys walking down the plank and took a step toward Wendy. His intention was to turn her face so that she should see the boys walking the plank one by one. But unfortunately for him and luckily for Wendy, he never reached her; he never heard the cry of anguish he hoped to wring from her. Rather his attention was caught by some other sound.

It was the terrible tick-tick of the crocodile, which was heard by all.

Every head turned in one direction, not towards the water from where the sound came, but towards Hook. They knew that the tick-tick sound concerned Hook alone. It was frightful to see the change that came over Hook. It was as if he had been struck motionless. He fell in a little heap.

The ticking sound was coming closer, and with it came the horrible thought, "The crocodile is about to board the ship!" Hook crawled on his knees along the deck as far from the sound as he could go. The fellow pirates were aware of his trouble, so they respectfully cleared the passage for him. At this hour of need, the only words that Hook said to his fellows were "Hide me."

At this order, all the pirates gathered around him, all eyes away from the thing that was coming aboard. They never thought to fight it as they had accepted it as Hook's fate.

When Hook was hiding from the tick-tick sound, it was then that the lost boys rushed towards the ship's side to see the crocodile. They were surprised to see that there was no crocodile present; rather it was Peter Pan, their own Peter Pan.

Peter signaled the boys not to utter any cry of admiration that might rouse suspicion. Then he continued to imitate the ticking sound of the crocodile.

Chapter 14

Hook's Last Battle

I n our lives we sometimes pass through certain odd things. Unknowingly, Peter also experienced such a thing that night. When we last saw him, he was stealing across the island with his dagger ready. He saw the crocodile passing but this time he didn't hear its tick-tick. Peter was surprised for a moment, but soon he concluded rightly that the clock had run down. Immediately, a thought struck his mind; he thought of using this for his purpose. So, he decided to tick, so that wild beasts should believe he was the crocodile and let him pass unharmed.

Peter ticked superbly, but with one unforeseen result. He never thought that the

crocodile could be among those who would hear the sound. The crocodile did hear Peter's tick-tick and followed him. I don't know the purpose with which the crocodile was following, whether it was for regaining what it had lost, or merely as a friend under the belief that it was again ticking itself. It will never be known, for it was a stupid beast.

Without any misfortune, Peter reached the shore. Then he went straight on for the pirate ship. As he swam, he had but one thought: "Hook or me this time."

He had ticked so long that he now went on ticking without knowing that he was doing it. Now, when Peter boarded the ship after frightening Hook and his gang, Ed Teynte, the ship's quartermaster came along the deck. Peter struck him with his dagger and Ed Teynte fell forward. Four of the lost boys caught his body to prevent any noise. Peter gave the signal, and the body was cast overboard. There was a splash, and then again, silence fell on the ship.

Peter immediately vanished into the cabin, and the pirates were no more able to hear the sound of the ticking; they were gathering up the courage to look round for the crocodile.

"It's gone, captain," Smee said, wiping off his spectacles. "All is fine once again." After this news by Smee, Hook came out of his hiding place. Once out of hiding, he listened so intently to his surroundings that he could have caught even the faintest echo of the tick. There was not a sound to be heard, thus, Hook drew himself up firmly to his full height. His hatred for the lost boys was roused more than ever, as they had seen him frightened. He thought of terrorizing the prisoners even more, though with a certain loss of dignity; Hook danced along an imaginary plank, grimacing at them as he sang:

"Yo-ho, yo-ho, the frisky plank,
You walks along it so,
Till it goes down and you goes down
To Davy Jones below!"

When he finished the song, he cried, "Do you want a touch of the cat before you walk the plank?"

When the lost boys heard this, they fell on their knees in front of Hook and cried "No, no!" so wretchedly that every pirate smiled.

"Fetch the cat, Jukes," said Hook, "it's in the cabin."

"The cabin!" The lost children gazed at each other, as they knew that Peter was hiding in the cabin!

"Ay, ay," said Jukes cheerfully, and walked into the cabin.

Hook had resumed his song:

"Yo-ho, yo-ho, the scratching cat,
Its tails are nine, you know,

And when they're writ upon your back ..."

What the last line of the beautiful song sung by Hook was will never be known; for the song was stopped in the middle by a dreadful shriek from the cabin. It wailed through the ship, and died away.

Then all of them heard a crowing sound, which was a signal for the lost boys but to the pirates it sounded creepier than the shriek.

"What was that?" cried Hook.

"Two," said Slightly gravely.

Cecco rushed into the cabin; the next moment he tottered out, looking worndown.

"What's the matter with Bill Jukes?" asked Hook in a terrified voice.

"He's dead," replied Cecco.

"Bill Jukes dead!" cried the pirates.

Of course, the lost boys were happy to hear this news. Hook noticed that and said to Cecco, "Go back and fetch me out that doodle-doo."

Cecco, bravest of the brave, trembled before his captain, crying "No, no!"

Hook scared him with the iron hook and said sarcastically, "Did you say you would go, Cecco?"

Cecco went, flinging his arms miserably.

There was no more singing as all waited for Cecco to return. They heard a death screech followed by a crowing sound.

No one spoke except Slightly.

"Three," he said.

"Who will bring me that doodle-doo?" thundered Hook.

"We will wait till Cecco comes out," roared Starkey, and the others agreed with him.

"I believe that I just heard you volunteer for the task, Starkey," said Hook, purring again.

"I'd hang before I go in there," replied Starkey.

"Is this mutiny?" asked Hook.

"Captain, have mercy!" Starkey sobbed in front of Hook.

Starkey looked for help from his fellow pirates, but they deserted him. Then, as he drew back, Hook walked towards him, his claw extended and with red sparks in his eyes. With a desolate scream, Starkey jumped into the sea.

"And now," Hook said, seizing a lantern and raising his claw with a threatening gesture, "I'll myself bring out that doodle-doo."

Now, all eyes were on Hook as he sped into the cabin. As speedily as he had gone, he came back, but without his lantern. "Something blew out the light," he said shakily.

Hook didn't want to enter the cabin again; the fellow pirates noticed this reluctance in their captain's behavior. The mutinous sounds broke forth once again on the ship.

Cookson cried, "This ship is doomed!"

The pirates were afraid now; Hook tried to awaken courage in them but his efforts were proving futile.

Hook tried to hearten them; but they turned on him instead!

"Lads," Hook said, "after thinking a lot, I have concluded that there can never be any luck on a pirate ship with a woman on board. Fling the girl overboard!"

"It's worth trying," the pirates said, and rushed to the mast where they had tied Wendy.

"No on can save you now, missy," Mullins hissed, jeeringly.

"There's one," replied the figure in the cloak.

"Who's that?"

"Peter Pan the avenger!" was the terrible answer.

As he spoke, Peter flung off his cloak. Then, it would have been considered foolishness if the pirates had not understood that it was he, who had been in the cabin. Hook was not such a fool, but he was awestruck to see Peter Pan alive. Twice Hook started to speak, and twice he failed.

In that frightful moment, we think, his fierce heart broke.

At last, he cried, "Tear him up!" but without confidence.

"Down boys! Get them!" Peter cried out to his army.

In a moment, a fierce battle began on the ship. If the pirates had kept together, they could have won. But they ran hither and thither, striking wildly, each thinking himself the last survivor of the crew, and then leaping into the sea.

By the end of the battle, Hook was the only one left on the ship.

A group of lost boys surrounded the pirate captain.

"Put down your swords, boys," a voice rang out. "This man is mine."

Hook found himself face to face with Peter. The others drew back and formed a ring around them.

For a long time the two mortal enemies looked at each other. Hook was trembling slightly but Peter had a strange smile upon his face.

"So, Pan," said Hook at last, "this is all your doing."

"Ay, James Hook, it's all my doing. I am sorry your plan didn't succeed" Peter replied.

"Proud and impudent youth," said Hook, "it's time to meet your death."

"Dark and sinister man," Peter answered, "I will get you."

There was no more exchange of words. Now, the swords clashed to give the final verdict and for a while it couldn't be decided who held the upper hand. Though Peter was a superb swordsman and moved the sword with great rapidity, Hook had the advantage of his great height and size. Hook thought to finish the fight by giving the last stroke with his iron hook, which all this time had been pawing the air. But Peter doubled under it and, lunging fiercely, pierced Hook in the ribs.

I hope I haven't forgotten to mention that Hook was repulsed by the sight of his own blood. Well, now I have told you. So, it happened that when Peter pierced him in the ribs, a stream of blood flowed from his body. At the sight of his own blood, whose peculiar color was offensive to him, the sword fell from Hook's hand, and he was at Peter's mercy.

"Now!" cried all the boys.

Peter always believed in fighting fairly, therefore he gave one more chance to his opponent for picking his sword.

Hook did so instantly, but with a tragic feeling that Peter was showing good form. Hook was now feeling a little afraid.

"Pan, who and what are you?" he cried, huskily.

"I'm Youth; I'm Joy," Peter answered; "I'm a little bird that has broken out of the egg."

This of course was a lie. But it was proof to unhappy Hook that Peter didn't know who or what he was.

Hook fought fiercely but he didn't stand a chance against Peter, who fluttered around him like a wind and pierced his body. Hook was fighting now without hope. Finally, lying on the ground, he saw Peter slowly advancing upon him through the air with a dagger. Hook abandoned the fight and jumped into the sea. He was unaware of the fact that the crocodile was waiting for him there.

And thus perished the dreaded pirate, Captain James Hook!

Among all the pirates, the two who reached the shore were Starkey and Smee.

Starkey was captured by the redskins, who made him the nurse of their babies; and Smee wandered around the world in his spectacles.

Wendy watched the fight between Peter and Hook, with glistening eyes. Once the fight was over, she started enacting the role of mother.

She praised all the boys, took them into Hook's cabin, and pointed to the watch, which said "half-past one!" The lateness of the hour was always the biggest issue with Wendy. She put all of them to bed, all but Peter who walked up and down on the deck, until at last he fell asleep by the side of Long Tom.

He had a bad dream that night, which made him cry in his sleep. Wendy remained close to him and held him tightly, whenever he cried.

A few hours later Wendy, with her children, had to start their journey to the Darling household.

Chapter 15

Reunion

N ow, it's time to return to the Darling household, from where three small children had flown away. Everything remained unchanged except for the kennel. It was not to be found in the nursery between nine and six o'clock. When the children flew away, Mr. Darling realized that he only was to be blamed, as it was he who had chained Nana up in the backyard, from the beginning; Nana had been wiser than he.

We know that Mr. Darling was a simple man, but he had a noble sense of justice and a lion's courage to do what seemed right to him. So, after the flight of the children, he went down on all fours and crawled into Nana's kennel. Mrs. Darling tried to persuade him, but Mr. Darling was firm in

his decision. He firmly replied, "No, this is the place for me."

Regretting his grave mistake, Mr. Darling swore that he would not leave the kennel till his children return. So, Mr. Darling sat in the kennel during the evenings, talking with his wife about their children and all their pretty ways. His respect for Nana had increased, therefore he would not let her come into the kennel, but on all other matters he bowed in front of her wishes. Every morning, the kennel was carried with Mr. Darling in it to a cab, which conveyed him to his office, and he returned home in the same way at six. He must be suffering horribly in the heart but he maintained a calm exterior even when the small children laughed at his little home. It didn't stop at that; when any lady looked inside the kennel, Mr. Darling lifted his hat courteously in respect.

Soon, the public came to know about the repentance to which Mr. Darling was subjecting himself. The heart of the public was touched, Mr. Darling's cab was followed by crowds, and charming girls scaled it to get his autograph. His interviews appeared in the best of papers and society invited him to dinner and added, "Do come in the kennel."

It was Thursday; a sad looking woman was sitting in an arm chair awaiting her husband's return. She was Mrs. Darling, in her nursery; there was no one to call her "mother". The gaiety of the old days was all gone now. I don't know what happened, but suddenly, she started up, calling her children's names.

There was no one in the room except Nana.

"O Nana, I dreamt that my children had come back." All Nana could do was to put her paw gently on her mistress's lap. They were sitting together thus, when the kennel was brought back. Mr. Darling put his head out to kiss his wife and asked, "Won't you play me to sleep on the nursery piano?"

As Mr. Darling was crossing the nursery, he said to his wife thoughtlessly, "Shut that window. I feel cold."

"O George, never ask me to do that," cried Mrs. Darling. "The window will always remain open for them, always, always!" After this Mrs. Darling went into the day-nursery and played.

After attaining pardon for what he had thoughtlessly said, Mr. Darling went to sleep. While he slept, Wendy, John, and Michael flew into the room.

They were glad to find the window open for them. It was more than they deserved. They dropped on the nursery floor, quite unashamed of themselves, and the youngest one had already forgotten his home.

"John," Michael said, looking at his surrounding, "I think I have been here before."

"Oh! Silly, it's your own house. Look, there is your old bed."

"So it is," Michael said, but not with much conviction.

"Look," cried John, "the kennel!" and he dashed to have a look at it.

"Perhaps Nana is inside it," Wendy said. But John whistled.

"Hullo," he said, "there's a man inside it."

"It's father!" exclaimed Wendy.

"Let me have a look at father," Michael begged, and he took a good look.

"He is not as big as the pirate I killed," he said, disappointedly.

Wendy and John were taken aback to see their father sleeping in the kennel. "Certainly," said John, like one who had lost faith in his memory, "I don't think he used to sleep in a kennel?"

"John," Wendy said, hesitantly, "perhaps we don't remember our old life as well as we thought we did."

A chill fell upon them.

At this moment, Mrs. Darling entered the room. Seeing her, they hid behind the door.

"It's mother!" cried Wendy, peeping.

"So it is!" said John.

"So, you are not really our mother, Wendy?" asked Michael, who was surely sleepy.

"Oh dear!" exclaimed Wendy, with her first real twinge of remorse for having

gone. "It really is quite time we have come back."

"Let us surprise her by putting our hands on her eyes," John suggested

But Wendy thought that they should break the joyous news gently. She had a better plan, "Let us all slip into our beds, and be there when she comes in, just as if we had never left her."

Mrs. Darling came back to the nursery to see if her husband was fast asleep. She noticed the beds occupied; the children waited for her cry of joy, but it did not come. She saw them, but she did not believe they were there. She had seen them so many times, the children in their beds in her dreams, that she thought it just another dream. She sat down in the chair by the fire, where she had nursed them in the old days. The children were bewildered by such a reaction; a cold fear of having been forgotten fell upon all three of them.

"Mother!" Wendy cried.

"That's Wendy," mother said, but still she was sure it was a dream.

"Mother!"

"That's John," she said.

"Mother!" cried Michael. He had recognized her now. .

"That's Michael," mother said, and she stretched out her arms for the three little children. This time her arms indeed felt Wendy, John, and Michael who had slipped out of bed and ran to her.

"George, George!" Mrs. Darling cried, when she could speak; Mr. Darling woke to share her bliss. Even Nana came rushing in.

There could have been nothing lovelier than this sight. There was some one watching a happy reunion, hiding at the window. It was none other than Peter Pan. He had had countless joys, something that other children can never know; but he was looking through the window at the one joy from which he must be forever barred.

You must surely want to know what became of the other boys.

Well, they were waiting downstairs to give Wendy some time to explain about them. When they had counted five hundred, they went up. But they didn't fly as they did in Neverland; rather they went up by the stairs. They thought this would make a better impression.

Once inside the room, they stood in a row in front of Mrs. Darling, pleading with their eyes to be accepted in her household.

Of course, Mrs. Darling said at once that she would have them. However, Mr. Darling looked gloomy and said that there wasn't enough space in the house.

"Father!" Wendy cried, shocked.

"We could lie doubled up," suggested Nibs, who was keen to live in the household.

"George!" Mrs. Darling exclaimed, pained to see her dear ones showing him in such an unfavorable light.

He burst into tears and then the truth came out. Mr. Darling was as glad to have them as his wife was but he thought they should have asked his consent, instead of treating him as a cipher in his own house.

"I don't think he is a cipher," Tootles cried instantly. "Do you think he is a cipher, Curly?"

"No, I don't. Do you think he is a cipher, Slightly?"

"No. Twin, what do you think?"

The consensus was that no one considered him a cipher and he was highly gratified for this. Therefore, he said, he would find space for them all in the drawing-room if they fitted in.

"We'll fit in, sir," they assured him.

"Then follow the leader," he cried, gaily.

Mr. Darling went off dancing in the house and all the boys danced after him. All of them found corners in the drawing-room to fit in.

As for Peter, he saw Wendy once again before he flew away. He deliberately brushed against the window in passing so that Wendy could open it if she liked and call to him.

That was exactly what she did.

"Hello, Wendy, good-bye," Peter said.

"Oh dear, are you going away?" cried Wendy.

"Yes."

"You don't feel, Peter," she said hesitatingly, "that you would like to say anything to my parents about a very sweet subject?"

"No."

"Anything about me, Peter?"

"No."

Mrs. Darling was keeping a strict watch on Wendy since she had arrived. Seeing her standing near the window, she joined Wendy in her talks with Peter. She told Peter that she had adopted all the other boys, and would like to adopt him also.

"Would you send me to school?" Peter inquired, craftily.

"Yes."

"And then I suppose to the office?"

"I suppose so."

"Soon I would be a man?"

"Very soon."

"I don't want to go to school and learn all grave things," he told her, ardently. "I don't want to be a man. O Wendy's mother, what if I wake up one day and find that I have a beard?"

"I think you will look handsome in a beard," said Mrs. Darling. "Come on in Peter."

"No, I don't want to grow up. Keep away, Lady."

"But where will you live?" said Mrs. Darling.

"With Tink in the house we built for Wendy. The fairies are to put it high up among the tree tops, where they sleep at night."

"How lovely," cried Wendy so longingly that Mrs. Darling tightened her grip.

"I thought all the fairies were dead," Mrs. Darling said.

"No, Mummy, you are wrong as there are always young ones who take their place," explained Wendy. "You see, when a new baby laughs for the first time, a new fairy is born, and as there are always new babies there are always new fairies. The mauve ones are boys, the white ones are girls, and all of them live on the tree tops in their nests."

"I will have so much fun," said Peter, with his eyes on Wendy.

"It will be rather lonely in the evening," she said, "sitting by the fire."

"Well, then, can't you come with me to the little house?" asked Peter.

"May I, mummy?" pleaded Wendy.

"Certainly not," replied Mrs. Darling, firmly. "After so long, I have got you at home and I don't want to lose you again."

"But he needs a mother."

"So do you, my love."

"Oh, all right," Peter said, as if he had asked this only out of politeness. But Mrs. Darling saw Peter's mouth twitch, and so she offered him this solution. She said, "I can allow Wendy to visit you, once a year during Spring time. She will help you in Spring cleaning."

This promise made Peter quite happy again. Mrs. Darling kissed him and he prepared to fly back to Neverland.

"Before Spring cleaning time comes, I hope you won't forget me, Peter, will you?" pleaded Wendy.

"Of course not," Peter promised; and flew away to Neverland.

Chapter 16

Epilogue

So, it was decided that Wendy would accompany Peter every Spring. And she did. Well, not every Spring, for you see Peter was very forgetful and had no sense of time, and so he often missed several Springs.

One night, when Peter came to take Wendy to the Neverland, things were completely changed. Wendy was now grown up into a beautiful young maiden and had forgotten how to fly. Besides, she was married and had a little daughter called Jane. Peter, who had remained unaffected by time and unaware of the changes that had taken place in Wendy's life, came to the nursery window and dropped down on the floor.

"Hello Wendy," he said, not noticing any difference in her.

"Hello, Peter," Wendy replied weakly, feeling quite helpless.

"Is Michael asleep?" Peter asked, with a glance on the little Jane.

"That is not Michael," she said quickly.

Peter looked. "Oh! Is it a new baby?"

"Yes."

"Boy or girl?"

"Girl."

Wendy thought that now Peter would understand her predicament. But no, Peter did not!

"Peter," Wendy, said, hesitantly, "Do you want me to fly with you to Neverland?"

"Of course; that is why I have come," he added a little sternly. "Have you forgotten that this is Spring cleaning time?"

Wendy thought it was pointless to explain to Peter that he had already missed many Spring cleaning seasons.

"I can't come," she said apologetically, "I have forgotten how to fly."

"Don't worry, I will teach you again."

"O Peter, no more; don't waste fairy dust on me."

Wendy now rose up to her full height.

Now, at last, a fear crept into Peter's heart.

"What happened to you?" he cried, shrinking.

"I will turn up the light," Wendy said, "and then you can see for yourself."

This was the only time that I saw Peter so afraid.

"Don't turn up the light," he cried.

Wendy turned up the light. When Peter saw her, he let out a terrible shriek. When she tried to console him, and stooped to lift him in her arms, he drew back sharply.

"What is it?" he cried again.

Wendy tried to explain things to Peter.

"I am old, Peter. I am more than twenty, I grew up long ago."

"You promised not to!"

"I couldn't help it. Peter, I am a married woman now."

"No, you're not."

"Yes and the little girl in the bed is my baby."

"No, she's not."

Peter walked towards Jane with a dagger in his hand. Of course he did not strike. Instead, he sat on the floor and sobbed. Wendy did not know how to comfort him, the job she once used to do so easily. She was only a woman now, and she went out of the room to think about it.

Peter continued to cry, and soon his sobs woke Jane. She sat up in bed, and was interested in him, as once her mother had been.

"Boy," she said, "why are you crying?"

Peter rose and bowed to her, and she bowed to him from the bed.

"Hello," he said.

"Hello," said Jane.

"My name is Peter Pan," he told her.

"Yes, I know."

"I came to take my mother to Neverland," he explained.

"Yes, I know," Jane said. "I have been waiting for you."

When Wendy returned after a while, she found Peter sitting on the bed-post, boasting about Neverland while Jane in her night dress was flying round the room, filled with joy.

"She is my new mother," Peter explained.

Jane descended and stood by Peter's side, as if supporting his statement.

"He needs a mother," Jane told Wendy.

"Yes, I know," Wendy admitted rather pitifully, "I know it very well."

"Good-bye," said Peter to Wendy, as he rose in the air. And little Jane rose after him. It was already her easiest way of moving about.

Wendy rushed to the window.

"No, no," she cried.

"It is just for Spring cleaning time, I will soon be back," Jane said.

"If only I could come with you," Wendy sighed.

"You see, you can't fly," said Jane.

In the end, Wendy let Peter and Jane fly away together. She stood at the window watching them going further and further till they were just two shining stars in the sky.

This happened years ago. Now, Wendy is an old lady. Jane is a married woman with a daughter called Margaret. Peter is still a boy and at every Spring cleaning time, except when he forgets, Peter takes Margaret to the Neverland. When Margaret will grow up, she will have a daughter, who will be the new mother of Peter Pan. Thus, it will go on till innocent children have faith in their dreams.

THE END